TEHUATL

SWORDS & WIZARDRY PLAYERS' GUIDE

Author: Tom Knauss
Additional Design: Tim Hitchcock
Project Managers: Zach Glazar and Tom Knauss
Editor: Jeff Harkness
Swords & Wizardry System Conversion: Jeff Harkness
Art Direction: Casey Christofferson
Layout and Graphic Design: Charles A. Wright
Cover Design: Charle A. Wright
Cover Art: Colin Chan
Interior Art: Julio de Carvalho, Adrian Landeros, Santa Norvaisaite, Terry Pavlet, Thuan Pham, Hector Rodriguez, and Erica Willey
Cartography: Robert Altbauer

FROG GOD GAMES
ISBN: 978-1-6656-0199-3

TABLE OF CONTENTS

INTRODUCTION

This product gives Swords and Wizardry players and GM's spells, equipment, and magic items designed for the Tehuatl expansion to the World of the Lost Lands campaign setting. However, you are free to incorporate the resources contained within these pages to any section of the Lost Lands or any other world of your choosing.

NEW SPELLS

The compulsion to create and innovate flows through the fiber of nearly every sentient being born and raised in Tehuatl. While most express themselves through mundane mediums such as painting, song, sculpture, and dance, some steer their imaginations toward the mystical arts. These practitioners devise new cantrips and incantations ideally suited for their unique environment. Their ingenuity appears in the new spells presented in this chapter.

CLERIC SPELLS

1st-Level Spells
Bloodbath
Counterattack
Detect Corpse

2nd-Level Spells
Cremation
Floral Bouquet
War Cry

3rd-Level Spells
Aura of Altruism
Flay Skin
Jaguar Spirit

4th-Level Spell
Sacrifice

6th-Level Spell
Palpitating Heart

7th-Level Spell
Volcano

DRUID SPELLS

1st-Level Spells
Bloodbath
Counterattack
Detect Corpse
Nohpalli
Pulque Infusion

2nd-Level Spells
Floral Bouquet
Heat Stone
Rust
Steam Bath
Wall of Smoke
War Cry

3rd-Level Spells
Falling Logs
Jaguar Spirit

4th-Level Spell
Magnetize

5th-Level Spell
Chinampa

6th-Level Spell
Flesh to Maize

7th-Level Spells
Black Hole
Uncoordinated
Volcano

MAGIC-USER SPELLS

1st-Level Spells
Babble
Bumble
Compulsive Step
Jinx
Numb
Slither
Stumble
Superstitious

2nd-Level Spells
Floral Bouquet
Parasitic Bond
Steam Bath
Wall of Smoke

3rd-Level Spells
Falling Logs
Flay Skin
Instill Madness
Triplicate

4th-Level Spell
Time in a Bottle

5th-Level Spell
Dance Miquiztli

6th-Level Spell
Palpitating Heart

7th-Level Spells
Black Hole
Uncoordinated

AURA OF ALTRUISM

Spell Level: Cleric, 3rd Level
Range: 30 feet
Duration: Immediate

This spell causes healing energy to radiate around the caster in a 30-foot radius. Every ally within range of the caster is healed for 1d4 points of damage. The cleric heals an additional 1d4 points of damage for every 3 levels of experience (to 9th level). Thus, at 6th level, the caster is able to heal 2d4 points of damage, and a maximum of 3d4 points of damage at 9th level.

Babble

Spell Level: Magic-User, 1st Level
Range: 30 feet
Duration: 24 hours

A creature within range of the caster finds it impossible to communicate verbally or in writing. The target must succeed on a saving throw or any words it speaks or writes come out garbled and incomprehensible. The target is unaware of the spell's effect, as it hears and sees its own words as it intended to say or write them. The target finds it impossible to cast spells or transcribe any documents, including spell scrolls and spells. Anyone listening to the target or reading its written words cannot understand what it is trying to say. Even spells such as *read languages* and *read magic* cannot translate the target's words, as it communicates with nonsensical sounds and indecipherable symbols. *Dispel magic* ends the effect.

Black Hole

Spell Level: Druid, 7th Level; Magic-User, 7th Level
Range: 500 feet
Duration: Immediate

This spell creates a tiny yet immensely dense object known as a black hole that appears at a point within range. The immensely powerful object pulls creatures and objects weighing less than 2,000 pounds within a 100-foot-radius toward it. Any creature that fails a saving throw is pulled toward the black hole and crushed within its event horizon, taking 1d6 points of damage per level of the caster.

Bloodbath

Spell Level: Cleric, 1st Level; Druid, 1st Level
Range: 30 feet
Duration: Immediate

This spell creates 10 gallons of blood to either fill an open container or to splash onto all creatures and objects in a 30-foot cube within range. The blood extinguishes exposed flames in the area and is identical in composition to the caster's blood. Each creature within the area must succeed on a saving throw or be disgusted and drop whatever it is holding. Disgusted creatures cannot willingly move closer to the caster and avert their eyes. Creatures that make a saving throw are still doused in blood but are otherwise not affected.

Bumble

Spell Level: Magic-User, 1st Level
Range: 30 feet
Duration: Immediate

After casting this spell, a creature of the caster's choosing within range must succeed on a saving throw or its initial attempt to interact with an object fails. This spell affects only a creature's first attempt to interact with an object rather than end an existing interaction. For instance, the spell can prevent the target from drawing a weapon from its sheath or picking a weapon up from the ground, but it cannot cause the target to drop a weapon it is holding in its hand.

The spell prevents the target from interacting with the same object for a longer period of time at higher levels: 2 rounds at 3rd level, 3 rounds at 6th level, and 4 rounds at 9th level.

Chinampa

Spell Level: Druid, 5th Level
Range: 120 feet
Duration: Up to 1 hour

This spell creates a one-foot-thick parcel of solid, dry land that springs into existence atop up to 1,600 square feet of water (an area 40 feet square, or 64 five-foot squares, or 16 10-foot squares). The parcel of land consists of bare earth devoid of any vegetation or life. The chinampa cannot cover any existing landmass at or above the water's surface, though any existing landmasses can be incorporated into the created parcel. At the end of the spell's duration, the caster can decide if the land becomes permanent. Otherwise, the land disappears when the spell ends.

If a creature is partially submerged beneath the water when the land appears, it must make a saving throw to emerge atop the dry land if it so chooses. On a failed save, the creature is pushed into the water beneath the dry land.

The land otherwise supports the weight of any creatures atop it, though structures made from stone or other heavy materials cause the ground directly beneath it to sink underneath the water's surface until it settles on the bottom.

Compulsive Step

Spell Level: Magic-User, 1st Level
Range: 30 feet
Duration: Immediate

This spell forces a creature to make a saving throw or move five feet into a space of the caster's choosing. The creature cannot be forced to move into a space with an obviously deadly hazard such as a chasm or open flames. The target continues to move in the chosen direction each round until it makes a saving throw to end the effect. Creatures immune to *charm person* are not affected.

The number of creatures affected increases at higher levels: two creatures at 4th level, three creatures at 8th level, and four creatures at 12th level.

Counterattack

Spell Level: Cleric, 1st Level; Druid, 1st Level
Range: Touch
Duration: 1 turn

The caster touches an ally who for the duration of the spell can immediately return a melee attack by a foe who attacks and misses. The spell ends once a counterattack is made.

Cremation

Spell Level: Cleric, 2nd Level
Range: Touch
Duration: Immediate

The caster touches a corpse or other remains, which is instantly reduced to a pile of fine gray dust that cannot be raised or turned into an undead. The creature can be restored to life only by means of a *resurrection* or a *wish* spell.

Dance Miquiztli

Spell Level: Magic-User, 5th Level
Range: 60 feet
Duration: 1 round/level

This spell compels up to 12 creatures within range to perform a frenetic dance routine. Each target must make a saving throw or feel an irresistible need to dance. The target incorporates the dance's violent, pounding motions into its movement, causing it to take 1d4 points of damage each round. Any attack on a dancer ends the spell.

Detect Corpse

Spell Level: Cleric, 1st Level; Druid, 1st Level
Range: Caster
Duration: 1 hour + 10 min/level

For the duration of the spell, the caster can sense the presence and location of humanoid corpses and bones that are not undead within 30 feet. The spell also allows the caster to identify the decedent's race and gender in each case. The spell can penetrate most barriers, but it is blocked by one foot of stone, one inch of common metal, a thin sheet of lead, or 10 feet of wood or dirt.

Falling Logs

Spell Level: Druid, 3rd Level; Magic-User, 3rd Level
Range: 120 feet
Duration: Immediate

This spell causes three 10-foot-long logs to appear vertically 50 feet up in the air above three spots chosen by the caster. The spots must be at least 10 feet apart and within a 40-foot radius of the first log's location. The logs immediately fall in a vertical line. Any creature directly beneath a log must make a saving throw or take 1d6 points of damage per level of the caster (higher-level casters create larger-diameter logs that do more damage). On a successful saving throw, the target takes half damage.

Flay Skin

Spell Level: Cleric, 3rd Level; Magic-User, 3rd Level
Range: 30 feet
Duration: Immediate

This spell flays portions of skin from a chosen target within range. The target must make a saving throw or take 1d6 points of damage per level of the caster (maximum 12d6 points of damage). The target takes half damage on a successful saving throw.

Flesh to Maize

Spell Level: Druid, 6th Level
Range: 60 feet
Duration: See below

This spell turns one creature within range into a maize plant. The target must succeed on a saving throw or it drops everything it is holding as its flesh transforms into fibrous plant material. Its legs turn into roots and a lower stem; its torso into a central stalk; its arms into leaves; and its head into an ear of maize. Its equipment melds into this new form. Creatures who succeed on a successful saving throw are not affected. A transformed creature can make a saving throw each round. If it makes three successful saving throws, the effect ends. If, however, it fails three saving throws, it permanently becomes a stalk of maize. These successes or failures do not need to be consecutive; keep track of both until the target accumulates the required number. *Dispel magic* also ends the effect.

Floral Bouquet

Spell Level: Cleric, 2nd Level; Druid, 2nd Level; Magic-User, 2nd Level
Range: 120 feet
Duration: Immediate

A flower bulb streaks from the caster's finger to a point within range and then bursts open to release floral aromas and pungent scents. Each creature in a 20-foot-radius sphere must succeed on a saving throw or be stunned by the sensory overload for 1d6 + 1 rounds.

Heat Stone

Spell Level: Druid, 2nd Level
Range: 150 feet
Duration: Immediate

This spell causes a 20-foot square contiguous stone surface centered on a point within range to instantly become searing hot. Creatures touching the slab take 4d6 points of fire damage unless they make a saving throw for half damage. Despite the stone's warm temperature, it radiates little heat and shows no outward signs of being hazardous.

Instill Madness

Spell Level: Magic-User, 3rd Level
Range: 120 feet
Duration: 1 hour

This spell causes a creature to succumb to madness if it fails a saving throw. While in the throes of madness, the target can only move or attack. It cannot activate magic items.

The target is free to decide whether to move or attack, but after it does so, it acts randomly. If it moves, it wanders in a random direction until it reaches its maximum movement or until it encounters another creature, obstacle, or obviously deadly hazard in its path. Roll 1d8 to determine the random direction. If it decides to attack, it can use only natural weapons or any weapon it held when it succumbed to the madness. It randomly attacks any creature within range.

Jaguar Spirit

Spell Level: Cleric, 3rd Level; Druid, 3rd Level
Range: 60 feet
Duration: 1 turn or until dispelled

The spell calls into existence a floating, spectral jaguar. The jaguar (3 HD creature with AC 6[13]) attacks a target chosen by the caster and deals 3d6 points of damage. The target must make a saving throw or be held and take an automatic 3d6 points of damage until it is freed. The jaguar does an additional 1d6 points of damage at higher levels: 4d6 points of damage at 8th level, and 5d6 points of damage at 12th level.

Jinx

Spell Level: Magic-User, 1st Level
Range: 30 feet
Duration: 1 hour + 10 min/level
A target the caster can see

receives an ominous feeling that something bad is about to happen. The target must succeed on a saving throw or be jinxed. A jinxed creatures suffers a –1 penalty to hit, damage, and saving throws for the duration of the spell. Additional creatures can be affected at higher levels: two creatures at 3rd level, three creatures at 6th level, and four creatures at 9th level.

Magnetize

Spell Level: Druid, 4th Level
Range: 120 feet
Duration: 1 turn

A metal object of the caster's choosing becomes a powerful magnet that attracts metal objects within a 40-foot-radius sphere. Any unsecured metal objects are pulled toward the magnet. A creature carrying metal items must make a saving throw to hold onto an object. Creatures wearing armor who fail the saving throw are pinned to the magnet. Anyone pinned to the magnet can make a new saving throw each round to pull away and move 20 feet from the magnet, but must make another saving throw in the next round if still within range. A weapon can be pulled free with a saving throw, but might be drawn back to the magnet in the next round if still within range.

NOHPALLI

Spell Level: Druid, 1st Level
Range: 90 feet
Duration: Immediate

This spell causes a four-inch-diameter cactus ball with one-inch-long needles to materialize and streak toward a chosen target. The caster must roll to hit. On a hit, the target takes 1d6 points of damage per caster level (maximum 7d6), and the ball sticks to the creature. The target takes 1d6 points of damage for two additional rounds unless the ball is removed.

NUMB

Spell Level: Magic-User, 1st Level
Range: 60 feet
Duration: 1 turn

This spell numbs a creature to pain if it fails a saving throw. The spell suppresses the target's pain receptors, causing the creature to believe its wounds and injuries are harmless scratches requiring no immediate attention. The target never willingly heals itself and refuses assistance from others. If an ally attempts to heal the target, the creature becomes enraged and attacks. The creature takes 1d6 points of damage each round it refuses treatment. The target can make another saving throw with a –1 penalty each round to shake off the numbness. Aztli priests sometimes use this spell on sacrificial victims to ease their suffering.

PALPITATING HEART

Spell Level: Cleric, 6th Level; Magic-User, 6th Level
Range: 60 feet
Duration: 1d4 + 1 rounds

This spell causes a spectral hand to reach into a living creature's torso and appear to rip out the creature's still-beating heart or other vital organ, which then instantly appears in the caster's hand. Blood and other bodily fluids gush from the creature's chest. The illusion is perceivable only to the caster and the target. The target must succeed on a saving throw. On a failure, the target believes the illusion is real and is stunned for the duration of the spell, taking 1d6 points of damage each round it is affected. When the effect ends, the target makes another saving throw. On a failure, the creature falls unconscious from the imagined pain.

PARASITIC BOND

Spell Level: Magic-User, 2nd Level
Range: 30 feet
Duration: 1 round/level

One target chosen within range must make a saving throw or become a conduit to heal the caster. Each round thereafter for the duration of the spell, the target must make a saving throw or take 1d8 points of damage. The spellcaster absorbs this damage through the bond as an equal amount of hit points. If the target succeeds on a saving throw, the spell ends.

PULQUE INFUSION

Spell Level: Druid, 1st Level
Range: 30 feet
Duration: 1 turn

This spell infuses pulque directly into a creature, which must succeed on a saving throw or become intoxicated, suffering a –1 penalty to hit, damage, and saving throws. A creature immune to poison is not affected by the spell.

RUST

Spell Level: Druid, 2nd Level
Range: 60 feet
Duration: Immediate

This spell causes a chosen metal object to rust if it fails a saving throw.
Weapons affected by this spell crumble into dust when they hit a creature or object, while armor and shields affected by the spell disintegrate when an attack hits the creature wearing or holding the protective device. The spell does not affect magic items.

SACRIFICE

Spell Level: Cleric, 4th Level
Range: 30 feet
Duration: Immediate

The caster selects one target, usually an ally.
The target of the spell takes no damage from the next attack that strikes it. Instead, damage that would have been dealt to the target is dealt to the caster of the spell instead. This spell must be cast before damage is rolled.

SLITHER

Spell Level: Magic-User, 1st Level
Range: Touch
Duration: 1 turn

A creature touched by the caster can crawl at its normal movement. It can also squeeze through small spaces a creature half its size would normally be able to maneuver through.

STEAM BATH

Spell Level: Druid, 2nd Level; Magic-User, 2nd Level
Range: 120 feet
Duration: Immediate

The spell creates a 20-foot-radius sphere of steam. Any creature in the sphere takes 1d4 points of damage per level of the caster, or half as much if it succeeds on a saving throw.

STUMBLE

Spell Level: Magic-User, 1st Level
Range: 30 feet
Duration: Immediate

This spell causes a chosen creature to fall prone if it fails a saving throw.
The caster can target additional creatures at higher levels: two creatures at 4th level, three creatures at 8th level, and four creatures at 12th level.

Superstitious

Spell Level: Magic-User, 1st Level
Range: 30 feet
Duration: 12 hours

A creature of the caster's choosing obsesses over superstitious rituals if it fails a saving throw. While affected, it dwells on real and imaginary omens around it. When the target misses an attack roll or fails a saving throw, it takes 1d4 points of damage. *Dispel magic* ends the effect.

The spell's damage increases at higher levels: 2d4 at 4th level; 3d4 at 8th level; and 4d4 at 12th level.

Time in a Bottle

Spell Level: Magic-User, 4th Level
Range: Self
Duration: Up to 1 turn

The caster saves a brief moment of time for future use. The caster can use the extra time to take an extra turn, even if he or she already took an action. The spell ends when the extra turn is taken or if the time limit expires.

Triplicate

Spell Level: Magic-User, 3rd Level
Range: 60 feet
Duration: 1 hour or until destroyed

The spell creates three illusory duplicates of the caster, which appear at unoccupied points chosen within range. Neither the caster nor a duplicate can occupy the same space.

The duplicates imitate the caster's actions but remain stationary. However, the caster can move one duplicate up to 20 feet in a round, but any duplicates outside the range of the spell are destroyed. A duplicate is also destroyed if it is physically struck, but spells do not affect it. One of the duplicates can also be designated as a point of origin for the spellcaster's magic, as if the spellcaster was standing at that spot. The duplicates last until the spell ends or the caster dispels them.

Uncoordinated

Spell Level: Druid, 7th Level; Magic-User, 7th Level
Range: 150 feet
Duration: Immediate

The spell overloads the central nervous system of a creature, disrupting its motor skills. The target takes 4d6 points of damage, or half damage if it succeeds on a saving throw. On a failure, the creature's movement is also halved, and for every five feet it travels, there is a 50% chance that the creature moves in a random direction. At the end of 30 days, the creature can repeat its saving throw against this spell. If it succeeds on a saving throw, the spell ends.

The spell can also be ended by *restoration* or a *wish*.

Volcano

Spell Level: Cleric, 7th Level; Druid, 7th Level; Magic-User, 8th Level
Range: 500 feet
Duration: 1 hour

This spell causes liquid magma from the planet's core to surge to the surface, giving rise to a volcano. The 60-foot-tall mound of molten rock and stone with a 10-foot radius instantaneously emerges from the ground. The volcano destroys any buildings in its path when it rises.

The small yet potent volcano belches pumice, lava, and pyroclastic gases within a 100-foot-radius sphere.

Each creature or object in the area takes 4d8 points of damage from the falling pumice and 8d6 points of damage from the falling lava. Creatures that succeed on a saving throw take half damage. When the spell ends, the volcano collapses in on itself and sinks into the ground.

Wall of Smoke

Spell Level: Druid, 2nd Level; Magic-User, 2nd Level
Range: 120 feet
Duration: 1 hour or until dispelled

This spell creates a wall of thick, black smoke up to 60 feet long, 20 feet high, and five feet thick, or a ringed wall up to 20 feet in diameter, 20 feet high, and five feet thick. The wall is opaque and cannot be dispersed by high winds despite being composed of wispy vapors. Creatures caught in the smoke take 1d6 points of damage per caster level and are blinded. Creatures who succeed on a saving throw take half damage and are not blinded.

War Cry

Spell Level: Cleric, 2nd Level; Druid, 2nd Level
Range: 30 feet
Duration: 1 turn

This spell whips the caster's allies into a frenzy for the duration of the spell. Up to three creatures within range gain a +1 bonus to hit, damage, and saving throws. At higher levels, the spell grants greater bonuses: +2 at 6th level, and +3 at 10th level.

New Equipment

The people of Tehuatl rarely sit still, physically or mentally. Their intellectual curiosity inspires them to constantly search for knowledge, while their ingenuity allows them to apply their newfound discoveries to aid them in their endeavors. A miniscule handful of technological advances are predominately confined to small corners of the island for various reasons, but the overwhelming majority of groundbreaking inventions spread across Tehuatl at breakneck speeds as local artisans and scholars devise innovative ways to enhance the original creation. The following chapter presents a broad overview of these wondrous devices ranging from armor, weapons, clothing, gear, and, of course, magic items.

New Armor

Steel and heavy armor fare poorly in Tehuatl's humid, semitropical climate. Over time, frequent rainfall and the moisture in the air take a toll on the ferrous metal's durability. Magical equipment ignores the ravages of rust, but being encapsulated within a thick shell of metal on a hot, sticky afternoon under the sun's relentless glare feels like a hellish torment. The island's weather conditions and environment generally lead most warriors to value flexibility and comfort over maximizing protection. Of course, some individuals choose the latter options, most notably the Firebrand dwarves of the Tepepan Mountains, the elves who still prefer chain shirts, and the Tlotls who closely guard the secrets of forging steel. Nonetheless, the bulk of the new armor and shields presented in the following section adheres to the principles of providing lightweight defensive options without compromising stealth and mobility.

Light Armor

This defensive equipment typically consists of thin, flexible material stitched together in layers to provide stopping power against projectiles and sharp implements as well as deadening the impact of bludgeoning weapons that strike the armor.

Ichcahuipilli. This two-inch-thick light armor resembles a vest designed to protect the wearer's torso from the neck to the hips against arrows and sharp blades. It consists of layers of cotton and vegetable fiber stitched together in a network of interconnected diamond-shaped patterns and then soaked in brine or another saline solution to harden the materials.

Tlahuiztli. Made from cotton or linen supplemented by hide or leather, this light armor covers the wearer's arms and legs and is worn over the ichcahuipilli. Unlike the basic undercoat, the tlahuiztli almost always boasts elaborate decorative features such as feathers, dyes, and other ornamental accoutrements. The armor's intricate and beautiful designs flaunt the wearer's wealth and status. The tlahuiztli presented in **Table 2–1** incorporates the underlying ichcahuipilli in its cost, weight, and game statistics.

Medium Armor

Protective gear falling into this category provides added defense at the expense of mobility. Supple materials are generally combined with more rigid, durable components to allow the wearer to better fend off attacks while not bogging him down with overly heavy gear.

TABLE 2–1: TEHUATL ARMOR

Armor Type	Effect on AC from base 9[10]	Weight[1] (pounds)	Cost
Light Armor			
Ichcahuipilli	−1[+1]	4	15 gp
Tlahuiztli	− 2[+2]	6	200 gp
Medium Armor			
Cipacahuipilli	−3[+3]	15	75 gp
Olli	−4[+4]	12	75 gp
Heavy Armor			
Ollixalli	−5[+5]	25	1,000 gp

[1] Magical armor weighs half normal

TABLE 2–2: TEHUATL WEAPONS

Weapon	Damage	Weight (pounds)	Cost
Melee Weapons			
Itztopilli	1d6	2	4 gp
Macuahuitl	1d8[1]	2	10 gp
Ollitetlacotl	1d6	1	35 gp
Ollitztli	1d6	1	40 gp
Tecpatl	1d4[2]	1	2 gp
Tepoztopilli	1d10[3]	6	25 gp

Weapon	Damage	Rate of Fire	Range[4]	Weight (pounds)	Cost
Simple Ranged Weapon					
Atlatl	1d6	1	30 ft.	1	1 sp

[1] Deals double damage on roll of 19–20; deep cut does 1d4 additional damage per round; second deep cut raises continual damage to 1d6; roll of 1 damages weapon and imposes −1 to-hit penalty; second roll of 1 destroys weapon

[2] Deals double damage on roll of 19–20; deep cut does 1d4 additional damage per round; second deep cut raises continual damage to 1d6; roll of 1 destroys weapon

[3] Deals double damage on roll of 20; deep cut does 1d4 additional damage per round; second deep cut raises continual damage to 1d6; roll of 1 damages weapon and imposes −1 to-hit penalty; second roll of 1 destroys weapon

[4] Shooting or throwing beyond this range is at a −2 penalty to hit. The weapon cannot reach farther than twice this range. Outdoors, these range increments are tripled.

Cipacahuipilli. This unusual armor follows the basic schematics for creating ichcahuipilli armor with a few modifications. Surprisingly, this armor is thinner than its lighter counterpart, but the flat pieces of hide and bone strategically sewn into the fabric adequately compensate for its lesser thickness. The armor's name comes from the flat sections of crocodile vertebrae and hide stitched into the material at vulnerable spots to improve toughness without adding tremendous weight and bulkiness. Most importantly, the armor's lack of metallic pieces or parts makes it immune to rust and suitable for druids.

Olli. Armor smiths combine latex and the juice from a morning glory vine to create a flexible and resilient material resembling modern rubber. Although typically used to create the tlatchli, clever innovators use the durable substance to protect warriors from injury. The lightweight suit includes a jacket and leggings. An inner and outer lining of breathable linen provides added comfort. While wearing this armor, you reduce any falling damage you take by 1d6 points, though you cannot reduce the falling damage below 0. Because it is made from plant-based products, druids are permitted to wear olli, and it is immune to rust.

Heavy Armor

Those willing to sacrifice mobility and comfort for added protection ultimately turn to heavy armor. This category of defensive equipment covers the entire body with hard, sturdy materials with the strength to deflect projectiles and even powerful blows from a melee weapon.

Ollixalli. One day, Atoyapaca, an innovative botanist and renowned jeweler, heated olli and combined it with ground quartz to enhance its strength. His bold experiment exceeded his wildest expectations, leading others to follow in its footsteps by adding other silica-based and sulfurous components to the liquified olli mixture. The delicate and laborious process of creating ollixalli is a tightly guarded secret confined to those who have the technical expertise and specialized equipment required to set the ollixalli mold. Unlike conventional heavy armor, a suit of ollixalli consists of a lightweight jacket and pants that protect the torso and limbs. Ollixalli has no metal components, making it suitable for druids and immune to rust. Because of the specialized training and equipment needed to create ollixalli, the armor remains extremely expensive and rare.

New Weapons

The lack of iron and steel has never hampered the island's weapon designers. The craftsmen who build implements of war emphasize creativity over components. Used properly, wood, stone, and other natural materials can be deadlier than a metal sword. Obsidian, a viciously sharp volcanic glass, takes a prominent role in this arms race. Its edges are keener than any steel blade, allowing the hard, brittle material to slice through flesh and bone with surgical precision. Yet achieving this incredible cutting edge also makes obsidian vulnerable to fracturing when it comes into contact with a hard object. Despite these breakthroughs, some of Tehuatl's inhabitants, most notably the Firebrand dwarves of the Tepepan Mountains, still place their trust in the forge's molten steel.

Atlatl. This easily made wooden device uses javelins for ammunition. To use this javelin launcher, you must place the javelin's butt into a cup, groove, or spur at the top of the atlatl. With your forearm perpendicular to your arm and the atlatl and javelin both parallel to the ground, you let the javelin rest atop your fingers while you hold the atlatl's base in the palm of your hand. When you are ready to release the javelin, you fling your forearm and wrist forward, which in turn pushes the javelin out of your hand toward the intended target.

Itztopilli. This axe has a wooden haft with a bronze head fitted into a groove built into the haft. The head is long and narrow, and its cutting surface is only slightly wider than the axe's flat back. The itztopilli's versatile design allows you to hack into flesh as well as chop wood with remarkable accuracy and comparable ease. Indeed, most woodworkers incorporate the weapon into a standard set of carpenter's tools.

Macuahuitl. Made from hardwood such as oak, this weapon resembles a long, flat paddle with obsidian or flint chips embedded into the weapon's edges. The insertion of these incredibly sharp stones gives the weapon unmatched cutting power at the cost of increased fragility. When you attack a creature with this weapon and roll a 19 or 20 on the attack roll, the weapon deals double damage. Furthermore, the creature struck loses 1d4 hit points each round due to the blade gouging a deep laceration through its flesh. The damage increases by 1d6 if you inflict another deep laceration during a subsequent attack. However, when you attack a creature with this weapon and roll a 1, you damage

the weapon. Your attacks with the weapon suffer a –1 to-hit penalty, and you can no longer inflict a deep laceration. If you damage an already damaged weapon, the weapon breaks, rendering it useless. *Ollitetlacotl.* This hardened rubber club is difficult to manufacture yet greatly valued among Aztli warriors for its lightweight punching power. Because of its unusual components and unique feel, the weapon requires more skill and training to wield than an ordinary club.

Ollitztli. Almost identical in its size, shape, and general appearance to the ollitetlacotl, this vicious weapon has an important added enhancement over its similar counterpart. When the olli starts to harden yet retains some malleability, the makers embed obsidian slivers into the weapon, riddling its surface with dozens of slightly raised spikes that puncture flesh like fine needles. Unlike the macuahuitl, which uses obsidian chips to form a contiguous edge, only tiny slivers of obsidian protrude above the weapon's surface, giving it a rough texture akin to a vine covered in tiny, fine-yet-rigid needles. Although the weapon lacks the ability to rip through flesh and bone like the macuahuitl, the tiny needles excel at delivering poison to a victim.

Tecpatl. Carved from flint or obsidian, this double-edged knife has a pointed tip and a decorative wooden, stone, or mosaic handle. Although an effective, close-quarters combat weapon, the tecpatl is predominantly used in religious rites and revered for its multitude of symbolic roles. When used in battle, it may open a deep laceration in the same manner as described under the **macuahuitl** entry (see above). However, because the knife itself is made entirely of flint or obsidian, the weapon irreparably breaks instead of being damaged when you roll a 1 on your attack roll with the weapon.

Tepoztopilli. This polearm has two components: a five- to six-foot-long wooden shaft carved from a single piece of wood and an oblong wooden head attached to the end of the shaft. The head ends in a sharp point, and like the macuahuitl, obsidian fragments are glued into grooves cut into the head to increase its deadly cutting power. When used in battle, it may open a deep laceration as described under the **macuahuitl** entry (see above). However, because such a blow requires greater precision than the macuahuitl, you inflict a deep laceration only when you roll a 20. Despite its surface area being much smaller than the macuahuitl, you still damage the weapon when you roll a 1. A second roll of 1 destroys the weapon.

Adventuring Gear

Like their armor and weaponry, Tehuatl's adventurers capitalize on the ingredients at hand to create potent concoctions and wondrous instruments to give adventurers more than a fighting chance in a dangerous world. These tools of the trade incorporate the designers' understanding of botany, astronomy, mathematics, and other scientific disciplines into these creations.

Table 2–3: Tehuatl Adventuring Gear

Item	Cost	Weight (pounds)
Cempohualxochi (vial)	50 gp	—
Chilli (vial)	50 gp	—
Coanenepilli (vial)	50 gp	—
Copal glue (flask)	100 gp	—
Cuitlapan	3 gp	5
Iyollo (vial)	75 gp	—
Kindling sticks	1 cp	—
Mictlampa	100 gp	—
Ollicactli	50 gp	—
Ollixima (vial)	25 gp	—
Passiflora (vial)	50 gp	—
Rust dust (vial)	25 gp	—
Tecuaniz (flask)	25 gp	—
Tlilitl (vial)	25 gp	—
Uictli	2 gp	5
Xochitl (vial)		
Zoyoyatic (flask)	20 gp	—

Cempohualxochi. A creature that drinks this vial of liquid made from marigolds gains a +1 bonus on saving throws for 1 hour.

Chilli. Made from the spiciest peppers on the island, this vial may be used as a food additive to enhance flavor and add heat to a dish when used in small doses — or it can be used to harmful effect. If you add the entire vial to food or liquid, the creature who eats or drinks an item containing chilli must succeed on a saving throw or be blinded for 1d6 + 2 rounds and unable to speak. Alternatively, you can splash the contents of this vial onto a creature within five feet of you, or you can throw it up to 20 feet to shatter on impact. When you splash the chilli or throw it, make a ranged attack against a target creature. A creature struck by chilli must succeed on a saving throw or be blinded for 1d4 + 2 rounds. A creature struck by chilli can still speak, unlike a creature who ingests chilli. *Coanenepilli.* A creature can apply or administer this salve to an injury or wound to heal 2d6 points of damage or to halt ongoing injury from a physical attack that poisoned the creature.

Copal Glue. When mixed, this amalgamation of cooked resin from copal and pine trees creates a strong and durable adhesive. When found, a container of this glue contains 1d6 + 1 ounces of the substance. One ounce of the glue can cover a one-foot-square surface. It takes 1d4 + 1 rounds to set. You can use the glue to repair a damaged or broken item (such as a macuahuitl or tecpatl). When applied to a surface that can be opened, such as a door, lid, or gate, the object becomes more difficult to force open, requiring an Open Doors check with a –1 penalty (minimum 1). The bond lasts indefinitely, though once a bonded surface is forced open, or a paired object becomes broken again, the glue is destroyed.

Cuitlapan. Primarily used to carry heavy loads long distances, this device consists of a wooden frame slung over the back. A cord affixed to the frame is then wrapped around the waist to keep the load secure, while a second strap loops just above the forehead for added balance. The cuitlapan has a volume of 1–1/2 cubic feet and a weight capacity of 50 pounds of gear.

Iyollo. A creature that drinks this delicious, chocolate-flavored drink experiences exhilaration and euphoria for one hour. The creature gains a +1 bonus to saving throws for the duration. *Kindling Sticks.* Without steel, most people use kindling sticks to start a fire. Enough sticks are in the kit to start 10 fires.

Mictlampa. Icons and symbols cover the face of this flat, round wooden board. The contraption has three movable hands corresponding to fixed points in the sky. When the hands are aligned correctly, it reveals your current position in relation to the four cardinal directions. *Ollicactli.* These sandals contain rubber padding and soles wrapped between two layers of leather for enhanced durability and cloth for added comfort. The shoes offer protection against the terrain and the elements, and reduce any lightning damage by 1d6 points.

Ollixami. This vial of black, clay-like material can cover a one-foot-square surface. Made from a mixture of latex, juice from the morning glory vine, and lime juice, it takes 1d4 rounds for this substance to set. The material can create a watertight seal or patch a hole in a canoe, roof, or other surface by forming it in the desired shape before it hardens. The bond can repel water and act as a sealant, but it lacks the adhesive strength to repair a broken object.

Passiflora. A creature that drinks a vial of this liquid made from passion flower gains a +1 bonus on saving throws against being paralyzed for one hour.

Rust Dust. The contents of this vial are spread onto an unattended manufactured object. The vial contains enough dust to coat a single object measuring one-foot square. If the object is made of a ferrous metal such as iron or steel, the dust chemically reacts with the metal for one minute. When the oxidation process ends, patches of orange rust appear on the object's surface. The item must succeed on a saving throw or crumble and become useless. The dust has no effect on magic items, constructs, or objects affected by a spell or magical effect.

Tecuaniz. The contents of this flask can be splashed onto a creature within five feet or thrown up to 20 feet to shatter on impact. In either case, the wielder must make a ranged attack against the target creature. The flask contains a mixture of herbs that distracts animals. If the target is a beast, it suffers a –1 penalty to hit and saving throws for one turn.

Tlilitl. A creature that drinks this vial of vanilla-flavored liquid with hints of chocolate gains a +1 saving-throw bonus against magical sleep for one hour.

Uictli. The wedge-shaped wooden or bronze blade attached to the end of this five-foot-long wooden pole is used to burrow into the earth to till, remove, or carve irrigation channels through soil and loose stone. A creature using an uictli can dig at twice its normal rate.

Xochitl. A creature that drinks this vial of vanilla-flavored liquid suffers a –1 saving-throw penalty on saving throws against magical sleep for one hour. Alternatively, a creature that drinks xochitl less than one hour before going to sleep falls into a deep slumber. A creature that normally needs eight hours of sleep awakens refreshed after only four hours of sleep.

Zoyoyatic. The contents of this flask can be splashed onto a creature within five feet or thrown up to 20 feet to shatter on impact. The wielder must make a ranged attack against a target creature. The flask contains powder made from the crushed seeds of the sapodilla herb. If the target is a mouse, rat, or wererat, it takes 2d6 points of damage from the poison.

Mounts and Vehicles

Beasts of burden are few and far between in Tehuatl, while wheeled vehicles are merely an oddity. Its people have undertaken little effort to domesticate the wild animals roaming across the island. Despite taming turkeys, ducks, and dogs, none of these creatures has the strength or stamina to haul wagons or carry large loads of goods long distances. Instead of expediting travel across Tehuatl, heavy wagons would constantly get bogged down in mud and standing water. Furthermore, the island's small size in comparison to Akados and Libynos does not create tremendous need or demand for a transportation network stretching across thousands of miles. Instead, commerce centers around the island's numerous waterways, including the Great Canal separating the Aztlis from the Poqozas. While most of Tehuatl's residents haul goods by canoe or by foot when traveling overland, there are some circumstances where people turn to a novel solution. Although not domesticated, the ilhuitecuani, a massive member of the pinniped family, can be used to lug an apanimacal, a hybrid aquatic-land craft, across relatively flat and stable ground. The following mount and waterborne vehicles are available throughout Tehuatl:

Acalli. This large vessel made from spruce wood measures 10 feet across and 75 feet in length from its upturned bow to stern. The waterborne vehicle can accommodate a combination of up to 60 passengers or three tons of goods. It takes a crew of six to 10 oarsmen to propel the vessel.

Apanimacal. The apanimacal combines several technologies to create a vehicle suitable for aquatic and land travel. The sleek vehicle is 30 feet long and 10 feet wide with an elevated deck atop its cargo hold and a tapered bow and stern. It can accommodate a combination of up to 20 passengers and 3,000 pounds of goods. It takes a crew of four to operate the vehicle. Its hull is completely flat, which allows it to float on the water or be pulled across the ground as if it were a sled. Some models have a series of ski-like rails that can be attached to the vessel's undercarriage while it is still underwater. The apanimacal is always propelled by an ilhuitecuani tethered to its bow.

Canoe. Carved out of the trunk of a single tree, this waterborne vehicle has an upturned bow and stern and is 15 feet long. It can accommodate three passengers, including its driver, or transport the equivalent weight in goods. The driver propels the vehicle with a long pole or paddle.

Ilhuitecuani. At a weight of nearly 5,000 pounds and almost 20 feet long, the massive ilhuitecuani looks more like a whale than an enormous member of the seal family. This carnivorous wild animal can be temporarily tamed or at least placated with abundant quantities of food — roughly 100 pounds of meat per day — and the proper coaxing. The ilhuitecuani is predominately used to haul the hybrid land-water vehicle known as the **apanimacal** (see above).

TABLE 2–4: MOUNT

Item	Cost	Move	Swim	Carrying Capacity
Ilhuitecuani	175 gp	9	15	800 lbs.

TABLE 2–5: WATERBORNE VEHICLES

Item	Cost	Speed
Acalli	4,000 gp	1 mph
Apanimacal	1,500 gp	2 mph on flat land or water
Canoe	150 gp	1–1/2 mph

MAGIC ITEMS

Courage and ingenuity alone can sometimes bring you only so far. When all seems lost, adventurers frequently turn to magic to even the odds and win the day. The sages and scholars who create magic items on Tehuatl frequently enchant readily available objects, items, and materials. The magic items in the following section embody such principles.

ARMOR AND SHIELD

ARMOR OF ELUSIVENESS

Warriors hoping to avoid being captured covet this armor, which appears to be coated with an oily sheen. This +1 armor (any type) grants the wearer an additional d6 for grapple checks. In addition, the wearer cannot be paralyzed or restrained by magic.

FEATHER SHIELD

This shield is made from tightly packed layers of eagle, falcon, or condor feathers bonded together with pine resin. Three times per day, the wielder can speak its command word to cause the shield to sprout wings and talons. The talons can slash or grab an opponent. A slash does 2d6 points of damage with a successful hit. The grab restrains a target if it fails a saving throw and can carry the creature up to 20 feet. The shield releases the target on your command. Any creature dropped takes 1d6 points of damage for each 10 feet it falls.

SERPENT SHIELD

The small, round *+1 serpent shield* is crafted from a wicker and wood frame covered with lacquer and serpent's skin and adorned with feathers and various patterns of color to denote the status of whoever carries it. The wielder gains a +1 bonus to saves vs. poison.

MAGICAL MISSILE WEAPONS

ARROW OF FLESH FINDING

The +1 arrow of flesh finding has the unusual ability to avoid striking inanimate objects in its path. The target does not gain any bonuses granted by cover or a shield. If the target's body is made of flesh, the arrow deals an additional 1d6 points of damage on a successful hit. Once the arrow hits a target, it becomes nonmagical.

STONE OF STUNNING

Made from hard rubber, these spherical sling stones are designed to debilitate rather than kill an enemy. When the stone hits a creature, the target takes no damage but must succeed on a saving throw or be stunned for 1d4 rounds. Once a stone stuns a creature, it becomes nonmagical.

MISCELLANEOUS MAGICAL ITEMS, LESSER

COCOA BEAN

This dried and fermented seed from the cocoa tree is usually found in a small pod containing 2d6 cocoa beans. When a seed is eaten, it heightens awareness, improves mood, and grants extra energy for 10 minutes, and the creature gains a +1 bonus to saving throws against being charmed, frightened, or confused. If two or more beans are eaten before resting, there is a cumulative 25 percent chance for each bean after the first that the target falls into a deep sleep for at least four hours. Usable by all classes.

SANDALS OF THE MITOTE

These durable sandals are made from maguey fibers and have woven fabric straps that fasten the shoes to the feet. Anyone wearing these sandals can move normally through terrains that would normally slow their movements. While the sandals let the creature walk through dangerous areas, it offers no protection against damage caused by these dangerous locales. Usable by: All classes.

TANGLED GOURD

This roughly spherical green, orange, or bright yellow gourd is three inches in diameter and weighs one pound. If thrown, the gourd rips apart on impact and fills the area with fibrous vines. Each creature within a 10-foot radius of where the gourd lands must succeed on a saving throw or be restrained by the vines. Creatures that enter the area must succeed on a saving throw to also avoid being restrained. Restrained creatures take 1d6 points of damage each round. A creature restrained by the vines can make an Open Doors check to escape. The effects last for 1d4 + 2 rounds. Usable by all classes.

TURQUOISE NACOCHTLI

Originally given to esteemed midwives, these ornate earplugs magically adjust to painlessly elongate and then fit inside the earlobes. Any spellcaster wearing them heals an additional 1d6 hit points of damage when casting *cure light wounds* or *cure serious wounds*. Usable by clerics and druids.

MISCELLANEOUS MAGICAL ITEMS, MEDIUM

DEATH WHISTLE

Three times per day, this whistle can be used to emit a horrific sound resembling hundreds of terrified voices screaming in unison in a 20-foot cone that is audible 400 feet away. Every creature in the cone must succeed on a saving throw or take 2d6 points of damage and become frightened (as per a *fear* spell). On a successful saving throw, the creature takes half damage, is not frightened, and is immune to the whistle for 24 hours. Usable by all classes.

EAGLE HEADDRESS

Eagle feathers adorn the sides and top of this headwear, while a long, slender beak covers the wearer's forehead. The wearer of this headdress gains a +1 bonus to ranged attacks. Once per day, the wearer can also cast *polymorph self* and transform into an eagle. Usable by fighters.

LUCKY FINGERS

These hideous trinkets appear to be a collection of 1d4 dried human finger bones held together only by hard, dry cartilage. They are usually found tied in a bundle hanging from a leather cord or stuffed in a pouch. Snapping one of the bones gives a character a +1 bonus on the next to-hit roll or saving throw. When snapped, the magic in that digit is released, rendering it worthless. Usable by: All classes.

Tlachtli Ball

This solid, rubber ball weighs nine pounds and has black and red swirling patterns painted on it. Three times per day, a command word can be spoken to cause the ball to fly in a 120-foot line. Each creature in that line takes 2d6 points of damage and is knocked prone. Creatures that succeed on a saving throw take half damage and are not knocked down. When the ball reaches the end of the line, it falls harmlessly to the ground, but the wielder can instantly summon the ball back to their hand. Usable by fighters and thieves.

Miscellaneous Magical Item, Greater

Box of Rocks

This small rectangular wooden box features decorative mosaic artwork depicting meteors streaking across the heavens on its exterior. It has no latches or hinges, yet it stays tightly sealed. The wielder must speak a command word to spill the box's 3d4 pebbles on the ground. Each pebble instantly fragments into a cloud of tiny rocks that swirl in a 10-foot-high, five-foot-diameter cylinder. Creatures that enter a swirling cylinder take 3d6 points of damage (or half as much with a successful saving throw). The rocks swirl for 1d3 rounds before they fall harmlessly to the ground. The box can be used three times per day. Usable by magic-users.

Cuacalalatli of the Beast

These wooden helmets are shaped into the likenesses of various beast heads. The protective device fits over the head and covers the top and back of the skull as well as the jawline. Anyone wearing one of these helmets gains the animal's abilities. The type of beast associated with the helmet determines its specific properties:

Crocodile: The wearer can slam its target for 1d6 points of damage.
Eagle: The wearer cannot be surprised.
Frog: The wearer can hold his or her breath for 15 minutes and gains a +1 to-hit bonus when fighting underwater.
Jaguar: The wearer gains a +1 bonus to attacks and damage against injured foe.
Monkey: The wearer can scale vertical walls (Climb 9).
Serpent: The wearer can slide through gaps half his or her size.
Usable by fighters and thieves.

Helm of the Ebon Serpent

Fashioned in the shape of lashing serpent's head, this light helm is crafted from lacquered wicker covered in black snakeskin. The wearer's face is framed by a gaping mouth with fangs in each corner. A crest of ebony-colored feathers adorns the top and runs down the neck. Three times per day, the wearer can spit venom 15 feet with a successful ranged attack. The venom does 2d6 points of damage and blinds an opponent. The target must succeed on a saving throw for half damage and to avoid blindness. Usable by fighters and thieves.

Jaguar Cloak

Stitched together from the pelts of Tehuatl's largest cat, this spotted garment also serves as a status symbol among the Aztli nobility. Anyone wearing it gains the following:

A Climb speed equal to its normal Move rate (fighters only).

A 20% Hide in Shadows bonus while hiding in grasslands, forests, or swamps (thieves only).

+1 to-hit bonus against a creature that is surprised and any successful hit does double damage.

Usable by fighters and thieves.

MASK OF SMOKE AND MIRRORS

This decorative turquoise mask is most commonly associated with the worshippers and priests of Itztliteotl. Deerskin straps attached to the sides of the mask keep it securely fastened around the wearer's head while completely covering the face. The mask lets the wearer see normally in fog, mist, or smoke. When worn in such an area, the wearer can also teleport up to 30 feet to an unoccupied space within the fog, mist, or smoke. Usable by all classes.

MASK OF QUIAHUITL

This stylized mask of lacquered ebon wood has long fangs and wide eyehole carvings that make the wearer appear to have oversized bulging eyeballs. The mask is topped with an elaborate headdress made from heron feathers. The mask lets the wearer see clearly through fog, rain, sleet, wind, and other forms of precipitation. Three times per day, the wearer can also use a gaze attack on a creature within 30 feet. The target must make a saving throw or be affected by *charm person*. Usable by all classes.

PUMPKIN SEED

The eyes of anyone eating a pumpkin seed glow, emitting a faint yellowish glow in a 20-foot cone for one turn. An undead or fiend caught in the glare takes 2d6 points of damage, or half as much on a successful saving throw. Alternatively, the eyes can pulse with a bright light for one round. Anyone caught in the pulse must succeed on a saving throw or be blinded. Usable by all classes.

SEAL OF MIQUITO

This strange stone vessel is circular shaped, about six inches in diameter and three inches tall. The sides bear thousands of ancient runes while a grinning skull is carved into the top. The seal separates into two pieces and feels unusually light (it is hollow). The wielder can force the soul of any humanoid within 100 feet to depart its body and enter the seal. The target must succeed on a saving throw to resist the pull of the seal. On a failure, the target's soul is trapped within the seal. Once used in this way, the seal cannot be used again for seven days. The seal can hold only one soul at a time.

When the soul is removed, the target's body falls into a catatonic state. If the seal is destroyed and the target's body is less than 100 feet away and is still alive, the soul returns to the body and the target regains consciousness. Otherwise, the target dies. Usable by clerics and magic-users.

TILMAHTLI OF FLOWERS

This white linen cloak features red, yellow, and blue flower petals stitched onto the fabric. When worn with the hood up, the flowers release a subtle yet perceivable sweet aroma in a 20-foot radius that beasts and humanoids find pleasurable and soothing. Any creature smelling the scent must make a saving throw or be charmed (as a charm person or charm monster spell). Usable by all classes.

TILMAHTLI OF THE OWL

This dark linen cloak bears the image of an owl with outstretched wings stitched onto the fabric. The wearer can grip the edges with both hands and raise and lower them to simulate an owl in flight. When done in an area of bright or dim light, the cloak casts an ominous shadow in a 20-foot cone. Each creature within the shadow must succeed on a saving throw or flee (as a fear spell). Usable by all classes.

WAR PAINT

Typically stored in clay jars, each container holds 1d3 applications of viscous pigments made from dyes and other colorful components. A creature can wear no more than three different colors of paint at a time, and only one color of war paint can be applied to a weapon. Any attempt to apply more colors fails. Each application of paint lasts for one turn regardless of color. The *war paint's* color determines its effects:

Black: The wearer is infused with a dark energy that deals 1d6 points of damage to any creature touched or struck.

Blue: A frigid chill courses through the wearer's body and causes frost to form on any weapon. The cold is harmless to the wearer and the weapon. This cold deals an additional 1d6 points of damage with a successful strike.

Green: The wearer cannot be restrained or paralyzed.

Orange: The wearer is immune to fear.

Purple: The wearer gains a +1 to-hit bonus during combat.

Red: Warmth radiates through the wearer's skin and causes one weapon to glow red-hot. The heat is harmless to the wearer and the weapon. This fiery weapon deals an additional 1d6 points of fire damage.

White: The wearer's weapon deals an additional 1d6 points of damage to undead and fiends.

Yellow: Energy surges within the wearer's body and causes one weapon to crackle with electrical energy. The electricity is harmless to the wearer and the weapon. The weapon deals an additional 1d6 points of electrical damage.

Usable by all classes.

POTIONS

BALCHÉ

This mildly intoxicating concoction is a mixture of tree bark soaked in honey and water. When found, a vial contains 1d4 + 1 one-ounce doses of the fermented liquid. When used, the imbiber gains a greater understanding of nature and cannot become lost or surprised while outside. The effects last for one turn. Usable by all classes.

XTABENTUN

This fermented beverage made from honey, tree bark, and corn allows the drinker to momentarily defy reality. When found, a vial contains 1d3 + 1 one-ounce doses of the prized liqueur. The imbiber experiences a sense of euphoria and gains a +1 bonus on saving throws for one turn. Usable by all classes.

RINGS

RING OF IRON

The Firebrand dwarves originally forged these expertly crafted iron rings as tokens of appreciation for trusted allies and loyal friends, yet over time they came to realize that the rings' usefulness outweighed their ceremonial purpose. The wearer is immune to fire and lightning damage. Usable by all classes.

RING OF PURSUING

This undecorated bone ring made from the vertebra of a large, predatory animal appears more fearsome when worn as a nose ring. The wearer can choose a creature within 30 feet and know its exact location for one turn. The targeted creature must succeed on a saving throw when it attempts to move more than 30 feet from the wearer; on a failure, it is magically restrained and cannot continue beyond that distance. The wearer cannot select a new target until the current target drops to 0 hit points or the turn expires, whichever happens first. Usable by fighters.

STAFFS

CHICAHUAZTLI

This *+1 quarterstaff* made from a long bone of a large beast or humanoid has a hollow interior filled with tiny shards of bone that rattle when shaken. While holding it, the wielder can expend one or more charges to cast one of the following spells: *bloodbath* (1 charge), *dance miquiztli* (4 charges), or *war cry* (2 charges). Usable by clerics, druids, and magic-users.

Staff of Wilderness Exploration

The wielder of this staff always senses the direction of true north. In addition, one charge can be used to learn the direction of the nearest natural hazard, such as quicksand or a volcanic pit, within 500 feet, although the dangerous obstacle's actual distance is not known. The wielder can also expend one or more charges to cast one of the following spells: *detect snares and pits* (1 charge), *find the path* (3 charges), *locate plants* (1 charge), or *speak with animals* (2 charges). Usable by druids.

Weapons

Macuahuitl of Revealing

The *+2 macuahuitl of revealing* does an additional 1d6 points of damage to shapechangers. If struck, the shapechanger must succeed on a saving throw or revert to its original form.

Legends claim the hero-gods used these weapons to unmask the emperor's serpent-advisors.

Macuahuitl of Quiahuitl

The *+1 macuahuitl of Quiahuitl* is carved from heavily lacquered dark wood and set with rows of gleaming obsidian teeth. The flats of the club bear engravings of a serpent coiled around a cornstalk set above a flooded plain. A tightly wrapped snakeskin covers a long wooden handle tipped with a collection of six heron feathers dyed orange and blue that dangle from a woven string. Three times per day, the weapon can siphon 1d4 hit points from the wielder as a sacrifice to Quiahuitl. When this occurs, the weapon deals an additional 1d6 points of damage on a successful hit.

Obsidian Dagger

Carved from a single shard of razor-sharp obsidian, this magical blade differs from the ceremonial daggers often used in sacrificial rites. Its blade fits into a cedarwood handle carved into the likeness of a pouncing jaguar. If the wielder rolls a 19 or 20, the attack rips open a vicious gash. If this occurs, roll another attack roll. On another roll of 20, the blade pierces the target's heart, killing it. If not, the blade deals 2d6 points of damage and the target's wound bleeds for an additional 1d4 points of damage until magically healed.